Fading From Forever

By: Britt Wolfe

Copyright © 2025 Britt Wolfe

All rights reserved. No part of this book may be reproduced, distributed, or transmitted in any form or by any means, including (but not limited to) photocopying, recording, or telepathic osmosis, without prior written permission from the author.

This is a work of fiction. Any resemblance to actual persons, living or dead, is purely coincidental—unless you feel personally attacked, in which case, maybe do some self-reflection. The characters and events in this book are entirely products of the author's imagination, and any similarities to real life are either accidental or a sign that the simulation is glitching.

Cover design, formatting, and caffeine consumption by Britt Wolfe. Additional emotional support provided by Sophie and Lena.

First Edition: 2025

Printed in Canada because books deserve a solid passport stamp too.

For inquiries, praise, declarations of undying love, or to request permission for use beyond fair dealing (seriously, just ask first), please visit: BrittWolfe.com

If you enjoyed this book, please consider leaving a review. If you didn't, well, that's between you and your questionable taste.

This Novella Is Dedicated to:

The warriors among us.

To those who have faced illness head-on and emerged victorious.

To those who fight every single day, carrying the weight of chronic illness with resilience and unshakable strength.

To those whose battles were too great, whose bodies could not keep up with the fire in their souls, but who loved and were loved so deeply that their presence will never fade.

You are seen. You are remembered. You are loved.

This story is for you.

Good Without You
Is Inspired by: *You're Losing Me*
by Taylor Swift

Since the release of Midnights, You're Losing Me has always felt like more than just a song—it's a quiet devastation, an unraveling, a slow, aching surrender to the inevitable. It captures the way love lingers even as life slips away, how the body and heart can wage two separate wars, and how grief begins long before goodbye.

This story, inspired by Taylor Swift's extraordinary words, is my tribute to those who have known the battle of illness—the warriors who have fought and won, those who carry the weight of chronic illness every single day, and those whose battles were too vast, too relentless, too cruel. It is for the ones who have fought with everything they had, and for the loved ones who stood beside them, holding their hands through every moment of hope, despair, and unwavering love.

To those still fighting—you are seen, you are strong, and your courage is immeasurable. To those who have survived—you are proof that light can break through even the darkest storms. And to those who were taken too soon—your love, your laughter, and your spirit remain, woven into the lives you touched.

I hope this story resonates with you the way You're Losing Me has always spoken to me—an ode to love that endures, to the echoes we leave behind, and to the strength it takes to hold on, even when letting go is inevitable.

Peace, Love, and Inspiration,

Britt Wolfe

Her First Battle
Two Years Ago

The exam room smelled like antiseptic and something artificial—clean, but too clean, like the scent had been scrubbed over something darker, something impossible to erase. The clock on the wall ticked softly, the hands moving forward with a propulsion that suddenly felt cruel.

Eve sat in a chair that was too stiff, her hands folded neatly in her lap, her wedding ring cool against her skin. It should have felt like a normal appointment. Routine. Sebastian had kissed her before she left that morning, his lips lingering on her forehead as he whispered, *It's nothing, babe. I'll see you for dinner.*

And she had believed him. She felt it too.

Now, Dr. Patel sat across from her, his expression unreadable in that trained, practiced way of doctors who have delivered bad news more times than they can count. He had kind eyes, a voice that was smooth and calm, but it did nothing to soften the next words out of his mouth.

Dr. Patel sighed, folding his hands on the desk. "Eve," he began, his voice steady but kind, "the results came back, and it is ovarian cancer."

The words shattered the air between them.

Dr. Patel's voice became a distant echo, muffled like sound traveling through water. Eve blinked at him, uncomprehending, her mind refusing to grasp the shape of the sentence he had just spoken. There was a speck of dust floating in the fluorescent light above his head. It drifted lazily, unaffected. The world had just shifted on its axis, but the dust kept floating. The hum of the overhead lights stayed the same. The clock on the wall still ticked forward.

Everything was indifferent.

Eve's chest constricted, the pressure sharp and suffocating. The walls of the exam room remained unchanged—pale blue, sterile, too bright. The floor still gleamed, the scent of antiseptic hanging in the air, the posters still pinned neatly to the wall, listing symptoms she had never thought to piece together.

Her body betrayed her first. The tremor in her fingers. The breath she forgot to take. The rush of blood crashing in her ears.

Cancer.

The word landed in the space between them, thick and final.

She stared at Dr. Patel, her throat too tight to speak, waiting—praying—for him to correct himself. To hesitate, to frown, to check his notes again, to apologize for some clerical error that had put another woman's name on her results.

But he didn't. The silence stretched. And with it, the slow, terrible understanding seeped in, cold and absolute.

This was real.

She forced herself to inhale, her breath shaky, her voice barely above a whisper. "Are you sure?"

Dr. Patel gave a slow nod, sliding a tissue box closer to her. Too close. Like he had seen this exact moment play out before, in this very chair, in this very room, with someone else who also believed this could never happen to them.

"I know this is a lot to take in. But I want you to know that we caught it early. We have a plan. We can fight this." His voice was firm, steady in a way that was meant to ground her, but she still felt like she was falling. "The next steps will involve surgery—likely a total hysterectomy, along with the removal of any affected tissue. After that, we'll discuss chemotherapy, possibly targeted therapy, depending on how much the cancer has spread. We'll take this one step at a time." Eve wasn't sure if his words were meant to comforting. Maybe he thought having options would make her hopeful?

She blinked, swallowing hard. A hysterectomy. Surgery. Chemo. The words stacked on top of each other, forming a wall too high to climb. "So... I'll lose everything?" she whispered.

Her mind thought back to all the times she and Sebastian had planned, breathing their dreams of parenthood out into the universe, replaying hundreds of conversations in an instant. They talked numbers and names, hopes and dreams. Now, all of that was dashed to pieces, never to be.

Dr. Patel hesitated. "Eve, I want to be honest with you. You will lose your ability to have children naturally, but the priority right now is you—keeping you safe, keeping you here."

Keeping you here. As if that was a guarantee he could give.

Her hands trembled. She clasped them together, pressing down hard enough that her nails bit into her palms. This isn't happening.

Sebastian should have been here. He should have been holding her hand, his warmth steady against her skin, whispering reassurances even if he didn't believe them. They had felt so sure, so certain that this was just a checkmark on a list, that she would walk out of here with a clear scan and a sigh of relief. You don't need me to come, he had said that morning, smiling at her over his coffee. You're healthy, Eve. They're just ruling things out.

She had believed him. She had felt it herself. This was just routine, another step on their journey toward building a family, even if it was late in life. Cancer was something that happened to other people, older people. It wasn't something that could happen to her, or to them.

And so, she was alone.

Her throat felt tight. "What's the survival rate?" she forced out.

Dr. Patel hesitated, just for a fraction of a second—long enough. He's picking his words carefully, Eve realized.

"If we treat aggressively, if the cancer is contained... the prognosis is good. We have every reason to be hopeful, Eve."

Hopeful.

Hopeful was a word people used when they didn't have guarantees. Hopeful meant that survival wasn't a promise, just a possibility. Hopeful meant she could still die. She nodded mechanically, not trusting herself to speak.

Dr. Patel leaned forward slightly, his voice softer now. "I know this is overwhelming. But you're not alone in this. Do you have someone you'd like to call?"

Sebastian. Her voice cracked when she whispered, "My husband."

Dr. Patel nodded, his expression kind but unreadable, and slid his business card across the desk. Eve barely registered it as she took it between her trembling fingers, the edges sharp against her skin. "Take some time," he said gently. "When you're ready, we'll go over everything in detail. You don't have to process this all at once." He spoke as if grief and terror could be neatly unpacked in stages. As if the moment she walked out of this room, the weight of the diagnosis wouldn't crush her whole.

She was on autopilot as she stood, her legs unsteady, as if her body was struggling to hold up the weight of the words still ringing in her ears. The hallway outside was cold, sterile, far too bright for a world that had just been turned inside out.

As she made her way out to the parking lot, she gulped at the cool air before leaning against the cool brick of the building to steady herself. Her hands trembled as she pulled out her phone, the smooth glass foreign against her skin. She stared at the screen, Sebastian's name waiting at the top of her messages. Just a tap away.

Her husband would be at work now, scrubbed in, his hands likely inside the open chest of some fragile, tiny body. Fixing what was broken. Saving someone's child.

She typed: We need to talk. Her thumb hovered over the send button. A wave of nausea rolled through her. No. That wasn't something she could drop into his world in the middle of his work day. She deleted it.

She tried again: Finished at Dr. Patel's. No. Too normal. Too small. A sentence that belonged in another reality, a different day, one where she walked out of this building untouched, unchanged. She deleted it.

Her pulse roared in her ears as she typed the words that had just been handed to her, as if writing them down would make them true. I have cancer. Her breath shuddered.
She stared at the words, her own confession blinking back at her in stark, merciless text. The truth sat there, waiting. Unmovable. It didn't feel real. How could it feel real when the world outside this building still moved as if nothing had happened? Cars passed on the street. People walked by, laughing into their phones. Everywhere, life was continuing.

But not for her.

She deleted the message.

I'm making your favourite for dinner tonight. She hit send.

The message delivered instantly, casual and weightless, as if it belonged to someone whose life hadn't just been upended in a too-bright room.

The weight of the diagnosis pressed against Eve's ribs, but the pain and confusion swirling through her mind weren't what she feared most. It was what this would do to him.

She would have to tell Sebastian. There was no way around it. They had been trying for a baby for four years. She could still picture the way his face had lit up on her 34th birthday when she finally told him she was ready. The excitement in his eyes. The way he had lifted her into his arms, spinning her in their beautiful kitchen, their laughter spilling into the space between them like something sacred.

And now, they had an answer. A cruel one.

She wasn't going to tell him because she needed comfort. Not because she wanted him to hold her, to soothe her, to carry even a fraction of this unbearable weight. She was going to tell him because he deserved to know the truth—because the family they had dreamed of, the future they had whispered about in the dark, had just been rewritten in permanent ink.

Still, she wanted to soften the blow. Even now, when her world was unraveling, Eve's first instinct wasn't to lean on him—it was to protect him. To put him first. To shield him from the full force of this devastation so that when she finally said the words, they would be gentler, easier, something he could swallow without choking on the grief.
She didn't want to interrupt his work. His work was important. His work was life and death.

So Eve, as always, would carry her pain alone just a little while longer.

Before slipping her phone back into her purse, she texted Madeline. She kept it brief, unwilling to let concern bloom before she had the words to explain it. Not feeling great. Going home. Talk later.

The lie tasted bitter.

The two of them had built Once Upon A Latte together—a boutique bookstore and coffee shop that had been their shared dream for as long as Eve could remember. A place filled with stories and laughter, warm light spilling onto old wooden shelves, the scent of espresso and paper wrapping around them like a second home.

Eve met Maddy on their first day of kindergarten.

Eve had been a timid, quiet little thing, standing at the bus stop with her hands clenched around the straps of her backpack, eyes wide with uncertainty. The bus had loomed in front of her, its doors hissing open, but her feet refused to move. The other kids had rushed past, climbing aboard in a blur of laughter and squeaky sneakers, but Eve had stayed frozen on the pavement, her heart hammering.

Then—a small, confident hand slipped into hers.

"It's not scary," a girl with wild, curly red hair and a gap-toothed grin had assured her. "I'll sit with you."

And just like that, Eve had moved.

Maddy had held her hand the entire ride, chattering away about how her older brother told her that school was full of cool stuff, like finger paints and story time and gym class, where you got to run really, really fast. Eve hadn't said much, but by the time they stepped off the bus together, she felt less afraid.

They had been inseparable ever since.

Through scraped knees and sleepovers, through their first heartbreaks and their wedding days, through the kind of deep, steady love that only a lifelong friendship can foster. Maddy had stood by Eve's side when she married Sebastian, tucking a tissue into her palm right before she walked down the aisle. Eve had done the same for Maddy, fixing her veil, whispering last-minute reassurances, then raising a toast so heartfelt at the reception that even Derrick, Maddy's husband, had teared up.

When Maddy gave birth to her first son, Eve had been right there in the delivery room, holding her hand when Derrick turned pale and had to sit down. And then again, for her second. And her third. "You're basically an honourary parent at this point," Maddy had joked once, holding her newborn against her chest, exhausted but beaming. "I should start putting your name on the birth certificates."

They had built Once Upon A Latte together, pouring their hearts into every shelf-lined wall and carefully curated reading nook. They had spent years wrapped up in this shared dream, a world they created together, where books and coffee and laughter existed in perfect harmony.

But today, it all felt distant. A life Eve had once been part of, but one that was slipping through her fingers.

Her fingers curled around the strap of her purse as she climbed into her car, closing the door against the crisp Bethlehem air. She inhaled sharply before starting the car, but the oxygen didn't feel like enough.

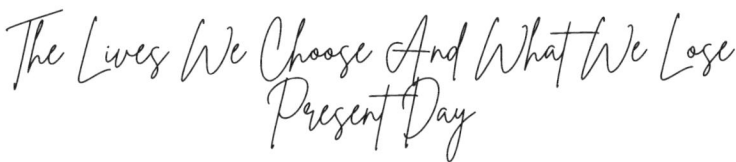

The Lives We Choose And What We Lose
Present Day

Now, Eve could still remember the weight of the grocery bags in her hands that day, the way the paper handles cut into her palms as she carried them inside the house. The quiet hum of the refrigerator as she unpacked the ingredients. The soft thud of onions hitting the cutting board, the rhythmic scrape of her knife against the wood, the scent of fresh thyme as she stripped the leaves from their stems.

She had gone straight to the market that day, slipping through the aisles in a daze, one foot in reality, the other trapped in the words Dr. Patel had said to her in that small, sterile office. Ovarian cancer. Surgery. Chemotherapy. The words had already burrowed inside her, taking root somewhere deep, but she had kept moving. Because if she just kept moving, maybe it wouldn't be true.

Sebastian's favourite meal—braised short ribs, slow-cooked in red wine until the meat melted at the touch of a fork, creamy parmesan risotto stirred in steady, patient circles, roasted garlic green beans crisped to perfection. She had made it a thousand times, had mastered it so well she barely needed to think as she cooked, her hands moving on muscle memory alone.

But that night, she had burned the garlic. She had stared at the blackened cloves, the acrid smell filling the kitchen, and felt something inside her crack. This could be the last time I make this meal without knowing if I will survive this.

She had scraped the burnt garlic into the sink, gripping the edges of the counter so hard her knuckles turned white, desperate to keep herself from breaking apart right there between the stove and the refrigerator, where she had stood a thousand times before, whole, untouched, unafraid.

She could still hear the sound of the front door opening, Sebastian's voice warm, unknowing. "Babe, whatever you're making smells unreal. God, I love you."

And she had turned to him with a smile, with a lie on her lips, with a secret curled inside her chest like a ticking bomb she dropped as they ate.

Tonight, she was making that same meal again. Tonight, she had another secret to tell him. This time, the bomb wasn't ticking, it was set to explode.

Standing in the same kitchen two years later, almost to the day, Eve let out a slow breath, her fingers trailing over the cool marble of the countertop. The light in this room had always been their favourite part of the house—floor-to-ceiling windows stretched across the entire back wall, flooding the kitchen with pale moonlight, making even the hardest days feel softer.

It was the reason they had chosen this house in Hanover Township.

Well—that, and the four bedrooms.

Eve had run her fingers along the banisters when they toured it, imagining tiny feet padding down the hallway in the morning, imagining toys scattered across the floor, imagining a nursery painted in soft colours. She had looked at Sebastian then, his eyes full of the same dreams, his hand warm on her back as he whispered, "This is the one."

They had signed the papers a week later.

They had believed in that future so completely.

And now, the nursery had never been home to anyone. The extra bedrooms were still empty, except for one where Sebastian had set up a treadmill he never used. The only children in their house were the ones they had lost before they ever had the chance to exist.

Eve pressed a hand against her stomach, against the place where her womb had once been. It was just an absence now. A space hollowed out of her, an echo of what could have been.

A cruel kind of death, the loss of something that had never lived.

Outside, the trees rustled in the cool autumn wind, their branches casting soft shadows across the kitchen floor. She could almost hear Sebastian's voice from that first night in the house, laughter in his tone, the scrape of his chair against the hardwood as he pulled her into his lap after dinner. She'd made him the same braised short ribs, parmesan risotto and roasted garlic green beans. His was a favourite meal that marked all their triumphs and now all their losses.

"If you ever leave me, I'm going to have to find someone who can cook like this." He had teased all those years before. Before the struggles of dreams unrealized. Before the cancer. And before this.

She had smacked his arm playfully. "Is that the only thing you'd miss about me?" She had asked, laughing. "Besides, if I ever leave you, it'll be to run away and open a restaurant in Italy."

"Okay, but I'm coming with you."

But now, she wasn't just leaving.

She was fading.

And where she was going, Sebastian couldn't follow.

As Eve cooked, she heard the front door open and click shut. Sebastian's voice, warm and familiar, drifted down the hall, laced with the kind of exhaustion that came with a long day at the hospital. "It's freezing out there," he muttered.

Eve turned from the stove, smoothing her hands down the front of her sweater. The air was thick with the slow-simmered richness of red wine and braised short ribs, the buttery warmth of parmesan risotto, and the sharp bite of roasted garlic. The house smelled exactly like it had two years ago, but she felt like a ghost moving through a life she no longer belonged to.

Sebastian shrugged off his coat, shaking out the cold before hanging it neatly in the front closet. His scarf followed, draped over the hanger, as he rubbed his hands together for warmth. His wedding ring caught the light—a glint of white gold, of devotion, of a thousand promises whispered against Eve's skin in the dark.

He turned to her, smiling. "Babe, this smells unreal." His eyes crinkled slightly at the corners, his gaze softening as it settled on her. "What did I do to deserve this?"

Eve inhaled slowly. Everything.

She crossed the kitchen in measured steps, greeting him with a soft kiss. It wasn't a kiss meant to linger. It was the beginning of a farewell wrapped in habit.

"Come sit," she said, leading him toward the large, round oak table where they had spent so many nights dreaming up a life they would never get to live.

Sebastian sat without question, stretching out his long legs, rolling his shoulders as Eve set his plate in front of him. His eyes lit up the moment he took in the meal, the nostalgia curling into his expression like a slow dawn. "You really went all out," he mused, glancing up at her. "Are we celebrating something?"

She swallowed, forcing a small smile. No. We're mourning something, she thought to herself.

Eve took her seat across from him, steadying her hands as she picked up her fork. She watched as he took his first bite, eyes fluttering shut briefly, a satisfied hum vibrating in his throat.

"You're spoiling me." Sebastian chuckled, shaking his head. "I don't know what I'd do without you." He reached for the wine Eve had poured him, lifting the glass. "Thankfully, I'll never have to find out."

Eve set her fork down with careful precision. Her stomach twisted as she folded her hands together, trying to brace herself for the impact of what she was about to say.
"Sebastian."

He looked up, mid-sip, brow furrowing slightly at the weight of sorrow in her voice.

She exhaled slowly. "I need to talk to you about something."

Sebastian lowered his glass, setting it down carefully as his fingers played absently with the stem of glass. His eyes lifted to hers immediately, his posture shifting, concern settling into the lines of his face. "Okay," he said, his voice gentle but alert. "What is it?"

Eve's chest ached as she looked at him—the man she had chosen, the man she had built a life with, the man she had survived so much with. The man she loved beyond words, beyond reason, beyond anything she had ever known. He took another bite of food, unaware that this moment—this ordinary, beautiful moment—was the last before everything changed.

She wanted to give him more time. More time to enjoy his favourite meal. More time to sit in the warmth of their home, with the soft glow of the pendant lights overhead, believing that their life together stretched out ahead of them, wide and certain. More time to be happy. But time was no longer something she could give him.

Her appointment with Dr. Patel that afternoon had made that brutally clear. There was an option, but it was cruel, merciless in its toll. The only medical path forward was paved with suffering, and it would not lead to survival. She could try. She could drag herself through more agony, endure more surgeries, more poisons pumped into her veins. But she wouldn't win. She would just buy herself more time to suffer.

And yet, she wasn't ready to go. God, she wasn't ready. But even more than that, she wasn't ready to tell him that he was losing her.

Her throat tightened, the words pressing against the back of her teeth like a scream she couldn't let out. She swallowed hard, gripping the edges of her chair as if she could anchor herself to this moment, to him, for just a few seconds longer. But the truth had already reached her tongue, heavy, inescapable.

"I don't want to keep fighting."

Silence.

And then, the shattering.

Sebastian blinked, tilting his head slightly as if he had misheard her. "What?"

Eve's heart clenched. "The treatments," she said, voice barely above a whisper. "The surgeries. The chemo. All of it." She met his gaze, willing him to understand. "I don't want to keep going."

Her eyes filled with tears. If they were talking about what she wanted, then she wanted to be healthy. She wanted a life untouched by hospital beds and IV drips, a life where she and Sebastian were still choosing paint colours for a nursery instead of thinking about palliative care options. She wanted to grow old with him, to wake up beside him on some distant morning when their hair had turned silver and their bodies had softened with time, not sickness. She wanted to want things that were still within reach.

But no one had ever asked her what she wanted.

The cancer had made decisions for her, sinking its claws into her body, its verdict absolute. All she could do was roll with the cards she had been dealt, though they had been shuffled against her from the start. There was no fairness here, no mercy—only the cruel indifference of biology, of a disease that didn't care how much love she still had left to give.

She blinked through her tears, her voice breaking on the last words. "I don't want this to be an ending." But it was. And, for the last two years, nothing she wanted had ever seemed to matter.

Sebastian stiffened. His fork scraped against the plate as he set it down too hard, the sharp clang slicing through the silence. "I don't understand." His voice was rough, fraying at the edges.

Eve swallowed, her hands trembling against the table. "I know you don't."

Sebastian let out a sharp breath, pushing his chair back slightly. His knuckles were white against the stem of his wine glass now. "Eve," he said, his voice steady but barely. "We've talked about this. We knew there'd be setbacks, but we're still in this fight. There are options, new trials, new—"

Eve shook her head, cutting him off gently. "I'm tired, Seb." Her voice cracked, and she pressed her lips together to hold the flood at bay. "I've spent two years trying. Fighting. Hurting." She inhaled shakily. "For you."

Sebastian's face twisted, his body tensing like she had struck him. "Don't do that." His voice was sharp, sudden. "Don't say it like that."

She flinched but held his gaze. "It's true."

"No," he snapped, shaking his head. "No, it's not." He laid his hands out flat against the table. "You're fighting because we have a life, Eve. Because we have plans." His voice cracked on the last word, his throat working as he tried to swallow the grief pressing against his ribs.

Eve's fingers curled into the fabric of her sweater, gripping it as though, if she held on tight enough, she could actually beat this. "Sebastian," she whispered, her voice barely steady. "I need you to see me."

"I do see you," he choked out, his eyes blazing with desperation. "I see you fighting. I see you strong."

She shook her head. "No." Her voice broke. "You see the version of me you want to see. The one who's still hopeful. The one who still believes in a future she's never going to have." She sucked in a shaky breath. "But that's not me. Not anymore. I'm too tired. I'm hurting and sick all the time," She tried to explain, her voice pleading.

Sebastian pushed back from the table abruptly, shoving himself to his feet as if standing might somehow change the reality of what had befallen them. He ran a hand through his greying, chestnut hair, his breath uneven. "We're not done," he said, as if saying it could make it true. "You don't get to just—just give up."

Eve's throat tightened. "I'm not giving up," she murmured, blinking through the sting of tears. "I'm letting go."

His hands curled into fists, his entire body vibrating with tension. "Eve, I—" His voice wavered, thick with something desperate, something broken. "I don't know how to do this without you. I don't want to!" He voice became petulant with defiance.

She swallowed back the sob clawing at her throat. "You'll learn. You'll be okay. You'll move on." Sebastian was only 45. He had a lot of life before him. Eve had no future left to plan for.

"No," he said, his voice breaking completely now as tears poured over his cheeks. "No, I won't." He pressed his fingers against his temple, his breaths ragged. "You have to keep trying. Please. We'll find something. We'll—"

"Sebastian." She forced his name past the lump in her throat, standing slowly. She crossed the small distance between them, reaching for his hands. He let her take them, but his fingers trembled violently against hers.

"I love you," she whispered, pressing his knuckles to her lips, lingering there, as if she could breathe the words into his bones. "But I can't keep fighting just because you need me to."

His whole body shuddered. "Yes, you can," he whispered, his voice so small, so shattered.

Sebastian clutched her tighter, as if holding her close enough could keep her from slipping away. Their bodies were pressed so close even breath had no space between them. His grip was desperate, frantic, his hands shaking where they touched her. "You have to," he choked out, his eyes searching hers like they could find another answer, another way. "You promised."

His breath hitched, his voice breaking as he threw everything he had at the moment, as if listing all the things they had yet to do could undo what was happening.

"We haven't been to Greece yet," he stammered, his words tumbling out too fast, uneven. "We're supposed to watch The Godfather together—you've never seen it! We were going to book that Airbnb in Vermont in the fall, remember? You promised." His voice rose with every word, shaking with anger, with grief, with the unbearable weight of helplessness. By the end, he was nearly shouting, his voice cracking as he flung accusations at a fate that wouldn't bend.

"You can keep fighting," Sebastian said with finality, like it was something she had simply forgotten to do.

Eve let out a ragged breath, her chest tightening, breaking, as she reached for him. Her fingers traced his jaw, cupping his face with a tenderness that made it all the more unbearable.

"No," she whispered, her voice trembling, almost crumbling. "I can't."

Her thumbs brushed against the tears on his cheeks, and she willed him to understand—to see her, not as the person he needed her to be, but as the woman who was already slipping away.

"And I need you," she whispered, her breath shaking, "to love me enough to let me go."

Sebastian's eyes burned into hers, dark and drowning, full of all the things he wanted to say. He shook his head once. Then again. Harder. His breath came in short, desperate gasps, his whole body trembling, denying it with every fibre of his being to somehow make it less true.

"I don't know how," he choked out, his voice unraveling, raw and wrecked. "I don't want to." And in that moment, with his grief pressed between them, neither of them could breathe.

Eve's chest ached with a grief so vast it felt like it might crush her, ending her life right here, right now. She squeezed Sebastian's hands, threading their fingers together, one last stitch in a life that was already coming apart at the seams.

"I don't want you to either," she whispered, letting her tears fall. "If it were up to me, we wouldn't be having this conversation at all. We'd be here, sitting at this table, our babies around us, their voices filling this house."

She glanced at the empty seats, and for a moment, she could see them. A little girl with Sebastian's dark eyes, a boy with her wild curls, maybe a baby in a high chair, banging a spoon against the tray. They would be laughing, talking over one another, lives so vivid, so real, she could almost reach out and touch them.

She swallowed hard, her gaze flickering back to Sebastian. His expression had shattered, his hands tightening around hers.

"We'd be talking about school projects and bedtime stories. About work and weekend plans. About stupid little things that don't matter because we would have had all the time in the world to talk about them." Her voice cracked; her vision blurred. "But we don't get that, Seb."

She blinked, and the ghosts of their children, their future, vanished into the hollow spaces left by the trying and failing to bring them into existence.

"All we ever did was hope," she whispered. "But someone else has been making the plans for us. And I'm so tired. I can't pretend that we get a say, or that we have any control anymore."

Sebastian let out a strangled sound—half sob, half gasp—like the air had been stolen from his lungs. His forehead dropped to hers, his whole body trembling against hers, his hands gripping hers so tightly, physically trying to hold her to this life.

But she was already slipping through his fingers.

The air was thick with loss. It pressed against Eve's chest, heavy as the silence the stretched between them, broken only by shuttering sobs and deep inhales of jagged breaths. Sebastian's hands trembled against hers, his fingers curling inward, gripping onto something he couldn't hold—her, their future, the life they hadn't had the chance to build together with so many cards stacked against them. His breath came in sharp, uneven bursts, as if he were drowning and had only just realized it.

Eve forced herself to meet Sebastian's eyes, her heart aching at the sheer desperation in them. "I spoke to Dr. Patel today," she explained.

Sebastian stiffened. His whole body went still, like prey bracing for impact. "And?" His voice was barely above a breath.

"There's one last option," Eve said, swallowing hard. "A surgery. A peritonectomy with HIPEC—heated chemotherapy, directly into my abdomen. They would remove the cancer, along with..." She exhaled sharply, trying to will the words past the knot in her throat. "Along with any tissue the cancer has touched. Pieces of my stomach. My liver. My intestines. Everything."

Sebastian's jaw clenched. "But they can remove it?" His voice rose slightly, catching on something fragile, something stubbornly hopeful. "That's good, Eve. That means there's still a chance." She had known he saw it as hope. She knew he would cling to it with everything he had.

Eve shook her head, already seeing where this was going. "It's not that simple."

Sebastian took a step back, as if putting space between them would somehow make what she was saying untrue. "What do you mean?"

"The surgery is brutal, Seb. You're a doctor. You know that," Eve said plaintively. They would be cutting me apart just to try and piece me back together. The odds of making it through are low. And even if I do—" Her voice cracked, and she squeezed her eyes shut before forcing them back open, willing herself to finish. "Even if I survive the surgery, I would be in the hospital for weeks. Maybe months. Recovery would be hell. And even after all of that, if it works, it just buys me time. The cancer will still come back. Again."

Sebastian ran a shaking hand through his hair. "But it's time," he protested.

Eve inhaled sharply. "Or it might kill me faster."

He flinched, as if she had struck him. "You don't know that."

"Yes, I do." She stepped toward him, pleading now. "Seb, even Dr. Patel doesn't believe this is a good option for me. He couldn't even tell me it was worth a try, and I'm just so tired." They pulled away from one another, Eve feeling like she wasn't being heard, wasn't being seen and Sebastian feeling like she was giving up when he still needed her to fight. He still needed her.

Sebastian let out a bitter laugh, but there was nothing humorous about it. "So, that's it? You're just deciding this? Without me?"

Eve's voice wavered. "No," Eve began, reaching for his hands. "I'm trying to make you see. I'm sick. I'm tired. I know you want to hold onto hope, but your hope is hurting me."

Sebastian took another step back, his hands running through his hair again. "I have been in this with you from the beginning. I have been fighting every single day, right beside you. Why don't I get a say?"

Eve's own frustration boiled over, cracking through the grief. "I'm telling you that my body is the one that has to endure it," she said, voice sharp with exhaustion. "I'm the one who has to wake up in pain every morning, I'm the one who has to drag myself to every appointment, every round of chemo, every scan that tells us the same goddamn thing—that it's not enough."

Sebastian turned away from her, bracing his hands against the back of on of their many empty dining chair as if he needed it to stay standing. His shoulders were rising and falling too fast, his breath coming in sharp, ragged bursts.

"I don't understand," Sebastian repeated.

Eve let out a shuddering breath. "I know you don't." Eve said again.

His grip tightened on the chair. "Then help me understand."

She exhaled, pressing a hand against her chest, as if that would hold her together. "I just can't keep doing this, Seb," she said finally, her voice barely above a whisper. "Not for you."

Sebastian turned back to face her, something breaking behind his eyes. "That's not fair."

Eve let out a soft, humorless laugh, brushing at the tears on her cheeks. "None of this is fair."

His breath hitched. "I don't know how to do this without you."

Her face crumpled, the weight of this moment pressing down on her like a tidal wave. "I know."

Sebastian was shaking his head again, over and over, like a man refusing to wake from a nightmare. "You can't ask me to let you go."

Eve reached for his hands, gripping them tightly. "I need you to love me enough to try."

The fight left his body in a single, broken exhale. He looked at her as if he was trying to memorize her, as if this was already goodbye.

Eve closed her eyes, pressing their foreheads together, feeling his ragged breaths against her skin.

They stayed like that, suspended in the cruelest kind of silence—the kind where love still existed, but it wasn't enough to save them.

The Hands She Held

Eve woke to silence.

Not the soft, comforting kind that stretched between two people who knew each other so well that words weren't always necessary. Not the kind that made a home feel warm, full, lived in.

This silence was empty.

Sebastian had left early. She knew it before she even opened her eyes, before she reached across the bed and found nothing but the cool imprint of where he had been. He hadn't woken her. Hadn't pressed a kiss to her forehead. Hadn't whispered "See you tonight, love," the way he always did before slipping out the door.

She should have expected it. She had expected it.

But somehow, the weight of his absence still pushed the breath from her lungs.

Eve swallowed, forcing herself upright. Her body ached—not just from the sickness, not just from the slow, merciless way it was hollowing her out from the inside—but from the sheer tiredness of it all.

The exhaustion of telling him. Of seeing the horror in his eyes as the words left her mouth. Of breaking his heart with a truth he wasn't ready to accept. He was losing her.

She swung her legs over the side of the bed, pressing her bare feet to the cold floor. The house felt different now. The walls, once so full of warmth and love and life, felt like they were already grieving for her.

Her hand reached toward her phone.

She should call Maddy. She had to tell her. But the thought of saying it again, of putting that grief into words again, of feeling it all break apart in real-time—she didn't know if she had the strength.

Still, her thumb hovered over Maddy's name in her contacts, lingering there like a secret she wasn't ready to release. She typed: Can you talk?

Then deleted it.

She typed again: I need you.

Deleted that too.

Her pulse thumped out an aggravating beat in her ears as she typed the words she needed to say but couldn't bring herself to send: I'm dying.

Her breath shuddered. Her vision blurred. The letters swam on the screen before she erased them, erasing the truth like that could make it go away. Eve was still staring at the screen when the phone rang.

Maddy. Of course. It was almost like she knew.

Eve hesitated before tapping accept, but she didn't have to say anything.

Maddy was already talking, her voice warm, full of life, full of everything Eve was about to lose.

"I swear to God, if Ben puts syrup on the dog one more time—" Maddy groaned. In the background, Eve could hear chaos—children shouting, something clattering, Maddy barely keeping it all together. "I swear, I birthed gremlins, not kids." She laughed, her voice strained from Maddy's youngest son, Chester, who was undoubtably in her arms.

Eve closed her eyes, just listening. Holding onto this moment, this normalcy. Because soon, everything would change.

"Eve?" Maddy's voice softened, the laughter fading into something steadier. "You okay?"

Eve opened her mouth, but her throat tightened, the words clogging there, refusing to come. She had spent her whole life speaking with Maddy—through every heartbreak, every joy, every moment that mattered. But this? This was the hardest thing she had ever had to say.

"No," Eve whispered finally.

The single word seemed to shift their entire world.

There was no hesitation. No pause. The sound of clattering in the background stopped, like Maddy had stepped out of the chaos, like she had dropped everything the second she heard Eve's voice break. That was who Maddy was to Eve.

"Tell me." Maddy demanded, her voice dripping with concern. It was not a question. It was a command.

Eve pressed her hand to her chest, gripping the fabric of her pajama top that had once fit her so well and now hung off her fading bones. Maddy had been there for everything. The first day of school. The nights when Eve's mother had been too sick to get out of bed, when Maddy had crawled out of bed late in the night just to hold her Eve's hand and to be with her in every moment that mattered. The mornings they had opened Once Upon A Latte, side by side, dreaming of a lifetime spent running the bookstore café they had built together. Maddy had continued running the shop once Eve became ill, taking on the bulk of the responsibilities.

Maddy had held her hand through all of it. But she could not hold her hand through this.

Eve forced the words out, one by one, breaking apart in real-time as she told her best friend the truth. Maddy did not interrupt. She did not tell Eve to stop, or wait, or breathe. She did not try to fix it, did not try to fight it, did not do what Sebastian had done—throw every possibility at her, grasping, begging.

Because Maddy knew.

She knew.

And that was almost worse.

There was no bargaining. No false hope. Just grief. Just the unbearable, deafening silence that followed the words Eve's seemingly tired old refrain: "I can't keep fighting."

When Maddy finally spoke, her voice was unsteady, wrecked.

"I can't—" A sharp inhale, a breath sucked through tears. "Eve, I don't—I don't know how to—"

"You don't have to know how." Eve swallowed past the lump in her throat, pressing her palm harder against her chest. "I just need you to love me through it."

A small, broken sound came through the line. A sound Eve had never heard from Maddy before. A sound that shattered her. "I love you," Maddy whispered finally.

Eve squeezed her eyes shut. "I know."

She didn't say goodbye. She didn't say I love you too. She didn't say anything more.
Because there was nothing left to say.

And for the first time in her life, there was nothing Maddy could do.

No hands to hold. No way to save her.

Just this moment. This unbearable, impossible moment.

Her Ghost Before Death

In the weeks following her decision, Maddy became more than a presence in Eve's life—she became a lifeline. She took over full responsibility for Once Upon A Latte, handling the café, the bookstore, the day-to-day operations that Eve could no longer bear to think about.

But she never let the business pull her too far away. Whenever she could be, Maddy was there.

Maddy would leave the shop early, leave staff to lock up, or slip away between rushes—just to be by Eve's side. She would crawl into bed beside her friend without a word, tuck the blankets up around Eve's shoulders the way she did with her boys at bedtime, and hum under her breath. She would rub slow circles against Eve's back when the nausea became unbearable, when the weight of sickness and sadness pressed so heavily upon her that it felt like she might slip beneath it entirely.

Derrick had always been the steadfast presence in Maddy's life, the kind of man who didn't hesitate when it came to his family. When Eve fell ill, Derrick didn't just offer support from the sidelines—he stepped fully into the role of primary caregiver for their three boys. He handled school drop-offs and pickups, made dinners, and managed bedtime routines with the same competence he brought to everything he did. He attended parent-teacher conferences, helped with homework, and navigated the chaotic world of playdates and weekend soccer games. By shouldering the bulk of parenting responsibilities, Derrick made sure Maddy could be fully present for Eve.

Eve loved it, and she hated it.

She hated that Maddy was sacrificing time with her family. That she was losing precious moments with her boys, her husband—her real life—just to sit at the bedside of a woman who was already so close to being gone.

"You should be home," Eve rasped one evening, her voice barely more than a whisper. Sebastian, as usual, had not come home yet, nor had he texted to let Eve know when he would be home.

Maddy didn't look up from where she was rubbing lotion into Eve's dry hands, smoothing the cracked skin with gentle care. "I am home."

The words undid her. Eve squeezed her eyes shut, letting out a broken breath, letting Maddy hold her hands even though it felt like something she did not deserve.

"I don't want to be a burden," Eve whispered. Her voice cracked on the last word, barely more than breath, as if even now, even here, she was still trying to make herself smaller, still trying to carry the weight of everyone else's comfort before her own.

Maddy's heart twisted.

"You've always been there for me," Eve continued, swallowing hard, forcing herself to keep speaking even as tears she could not spare welled in her eyes. "You've done so much for me, Maddy, and I—"

Her voice faltered. She couldn't bring herself to say more. She couldn't find the words to capture the depth of her gratitude, to articulate how much Maddy's presence had saved her, to put into words what it meant to be loved so fiercely at the end of everything.

Maddy reached for a tissue, dabbing at Eve's damp cheeks with careful, practiced tenderness. Then, she brushed her fingers through Eve's sweat-dampened hair, the way she had done a thousand times before—when they were kids, when Eve had been sick with the flu, when Eve had sobbed into her lap the night her mother passed away.

"You are not a burden," Maddy said softly, her voice steady even as her throat burned with the ache of impending loss. She smoothed Eve's hair away from her face. "You are my best friend. And it is a privilege to be here for you. It always has been."

Eve's lip trembled.

Maddy saw it—the way she swallowed down her emotions like she didn't deserve to feel them, like she was inconveniencing the people who loved her by dying, and Maddy's chest tightened.

She had watched Eve bend and bend and bend, shaping herself around everyone else's needs, giving until there was nothing left for herself. And even now—even now, when she was dying, she was still apologizing for it.

Maddy let out a shaking breath, her own tears brimming.

"I have watched you do and be everything for everyone," she murmured, her fingers still stroking Eve's hair. "You have never once put yourself first. Not once. You carry everyone. You hold everyone. You love so fiercely, so completely, and you do it like it costs you nothing."

Eve's breath hitched, but Maddy kept going.

"I saw it in you so many years ago. That's why I stayed, why I fought to be in your life, why I've always tried to make sure that there was someone beside you, holding you up, because God knows you would never ask for it." Maddy's voice broke, her tears slipping free.

"You've been people-pleasing your whole life like it's the terminal disease you are inflicted with," Maddy said.

Eve let out a sharp, shattered sound—something between a laugh and a sob.
Maddy cupped her face, thumbs sweeping away fresh tears. "And even now," she whispered, her voice thick, "you act like this is something you're doing to us. Like this is something you've done for yourself, like dying is a choice you made that we're all just supposed to endure. But Eve, my best friend—"

Her voice wavered.

"You carry the weight of it so apologetically, it's like—" Maddy let out a trembling breath, pressing her lips together to keep from breaking completely.

Eve watched her, eyes wet, wide, silent.

"You act like me being here for you, like me holding onto you, is a favour." Maddy let out a small, broken sound, shaking her head. "But it is our privilege."

The words shattered between them. Maddy let out a sharp, wrecked sob, pressing her forehead against Eve's, holding on, holding on, holding on.

If Maddy was the one holding onto her, Sebastian was the one letting go. He didn't speak to her unless he had to. When he did, it was in short, clipped sentences that held no trace of warmth, no hint of the man who used to kiss her fingertips just for the sake of it, who used to press his forehead to hers and murmur "Forever, okay?" as if saying it made it true.

Now, he barely looked at her. Most days, he left before she woke, and when he came home, he moved through the house like she wasn't even there. Like she was already a ghost, haunting the life they had built over the last 20 years together.

Eve tried to reach for him. Once, in the middle of the night, she had stirred to find him sitting on the edge of the bed, his back to her, his hands clenched into fists on his knees.

"Seb?" she had whispered, reaching out, her fingertips brushing against his spine. He had flinched.

Not visibly. Not violently. But enough for Eve to notice.

At her touch, Sebastian had exhaled sharply, like her touch burned, before standing and walking out of the bedroom without a word.

Eve had curled into herself after that, swallowing the sob that tried to claw its way up her throat.

Since then, he hadn't slept beside her. Most nights, he stayed in one of their many spare bedrooms, though he seemed to gravitate toward the one closest to theirs—the room they had painted yellow when those two pink lines had first appeared. Before Eve's period arrived with a vengeance, the cramping so sharp and unbearable that even she knew something was wrong. Before the doctor gently confirmed what they had already knew—a loss so early it barely had a name, but one that had gutted them all the same.

Eve didn't know which hurt more: that he was running from her, or that he was running to the memory of what they had lost.

She wanted to beg him to see her. Beg him to love her the way he used to. To give her something, anything that made her feel real again.

But she knew—deep down, in the aching marrow of her bones—that Sebastian could not love her the way he had before.

Because she was dying. Because he was losing her.

What Remains When Goodbye begins

Sebastian came home late. Again.

Eve heard the front door open, the shuffle of his boots against the hardwood, the muffled sigh as he shrugged off his coat. She had set his plate aside to keep it warm, waiting, always waiting—even when waiting felt like an act of futility.

She had no appetite. She hadn't had one in weeks. But she still sat at the table, hands wrapped around a lukewarm mug of green tea, staring at the flickering candle she had lit in some small, desperate attempt to make tonight feel normal.

It wasn't.

Sebastian walked into the kitchen, pausing as he took in the spread on the table. His favourite—braised short ribs, parmesan risotto, roasted garlic green beans. The same meal she had made the night she told him she had cancer. The same meal she had made the night she told him she wasn't going to fight anymore.

His expression didn't shift, but she saw it—the flicker of recognition, the way his throat bobbed as he swallowed down whatever emotion he was choking on.

"I already made you up a plate," Eve said softly.

Sebastian nodded, his movements stiff, his body wound so tight he looked like he might snap under the weight of himself. He stepped forward, rolling up his sleeves with the same absent-minded precision he used after long hours at the hospital. "You didn't have to do this."

Eve offered him a small, tired smile. "I wanted to." She needed to. Taking care of him had always been second nature, as instinctive as breathing. Maddy was right—she was a people pleaser, always had been. It was terminal. But this wasn't about obligation, or routine, or trying to fill the silence with something that resembled normalcy.

This was love. This was all she had left to give.

Her body was failing her. The days were slipping through her fingers like sand, impossible to hold, impossible to slow. But she could still do this. She could still love him the way she always had—through food, through warmth, through the simple, quiet acts of care that had stitched their life together over the years. She could still make his favourite meal. She could still set the table. She could still pour what little remained of herself into the man she had loved for what felt like a thousand lifetimes.

Sebastian didn't argue. Didn't say thank you. Just walked to the table where his place was set, sat down, and began to eat.

Eve watched from across the table, her fingers curled around the edge of her mug. The only sound in the room was the soft clink of Sebastian's fork against ceramic, the slow, steady rhythm of a life continuing even as hers was slipping away.

For a long time, there was only silence.

Sebastian ate.

Eve watched him eat.

She traced the lines of his face with her tired eyes—the tightness in his jaw, the exhaustion that lived permanently beneath his eyes, the way his shoulders remained tense as if he were bracing for an impact that had already come. She wanted to reach across the table, to lace her fingers through his, to feel something—but there was a distance between them now that no meal, no gesture, no act of love could bridge.

Finally, she couldn't take it anymore.

"What can I do to make this easier for you?" she asked, her voice barely above a whisper.

Sebastian didn't look up.

Eve inhaled deeply, forcing herself to stay steady. "I know this isn't fair," she continued, her words careful, deliberate. "I know you're angry. I know you don't want to do this—"

The sharp scrape of metal against porcelain cut through the air as Sebastian set his fork down abruptly.

"I'm not angry," he said flatly.

Eve's chest tightened. "Sebastian—"

"I'm not angry," he repeated, reaching for his glass of wine—the one she had poured for him—and taking a long, deliberate sip. His hand was steady. His voice was steady.
Everything about him was steady in a way that told her it was a lie.

Eve swallowed hard. "Then what are you?"

Sebastian exhaled sharply, shaking his head. "I don't know what you want me to say, Eve."

"I want the truth." Her voice wavered, thick with the grief she hadn't yet let herself feel. "I want you to talk to me. I want you to look at me the way you used to."

She blinked back tears, her vision swimming.

And for just a second, his gaze flickered to hers.

Just long enough for her to see everything he wasn't saying. The grief. The helplessness. The unbearable weight of losing her while she was still here.

But then Sebastian blinked. And it was gone.

He pushed his chair back and stood, taking his plate with him. "Everything's fine," he murmured.

Eve let out a slow, uneven breath. "No, it's not."

Sebastian didn't answer. He walked to the sink, rinsed his plate under the faucet, and set it down with deliberate care. Then, without another word, he left the kitchen, heading up the stairs.

Eve stared after him, her chest tightening, her hands trembling in her lap.

She loved him. God, she loved him. She had spent her whole life putting other people first, putting him first. Being the strong one. The steady one. The one who carried everyone else's pain before allowing herself to feel her own.

And now, at the end of everything, she just wanted to be brave for him. She wanted to be his bravest soldier. To carry him through this.

But what did it mean to be brave, when every battle was already lost?

The weight of exhaustion pressed down on Eve as she climbed the stairs, following after Sebastian. Her body slow, each step an effort she had to consciously force herself through. The ache in her bones was deeper tonight—more than pain, more than fatigue. It was something final, something she could feel in the marrow of her existence.

She paused on the landing, one hand gripping the banister as she tried to steady herself, to gather the energy to make it down the hall. Her lungs pulled in air, but it didn't feel like enough.

She squeezed her eyes shut, willing the house to stop spinning, willing her body to hold on just a little longer. When she finally opened them, she saw the light spilling from the open doorway down the hall.

Sebastian was in the would-be nursery. Of course he was.

She knew before she even stepped forward that she'd find him sitting on that goddamn bed—the one they kept made up for guests that had replaced the crib. The room that was supposed to hold their dreams, their future, their family had instead become a place where Sebastian went when he couldn't bear to be near her.

Tonight, it was where he had fled once again.

Her fingers curled into her palm, nails pressing into skin. She forced herself to move. When she reached the doorway, she found him sitting on the edge of the bed, his elbows braced against his knees, his hands clenched together so tightly his knuckles were white.

His back was to her, his breathing slow, too even. The room was dim, the moonlight filtering through the curtains, casting pale shadows over the soft yellow walls.

Walls they had painted together - Walls that had been meant to witness lullabies, bedtime stories, sleepy morning giggles.

Instead, they had borne witness to grief, to distance, to a love unraveling under loss.

Eve leaned against the doorframe, her fingers drifting to her mouth. Her nails—already bitten down to nothing—pressed against her lips, her teeth sinking into the edges of one before she caught herself.

She let out a slow breath. "You're going to regret this," she said softly.

Sebastian didn't move. "Regret what?" His voice was tired, hollow.

"Pulling away from me," Eve replied.

That made him laugh—a sharp, bitter sound that held no humour. "Pulling away from you?" He turned then, his eyes dark, hollowed with exhaustion and something else—something dangerously close to rage.

Eve steeled herself.

"You're the one leaving, Eve," he said, his voice breaking on her name. "You're the one choosing this."

Her breath hitched. "I'm not choosing—"

"Yes, you are!" He was on his feet now, towering over her, his face contorted with something raw, something jagged. "You decided. You looked me in the eye, and you decided that you were done. You decided we were done. You didn't ask me. You told me!" He bellowed.

Eve swallowed hard, forcing herself to stand her ground. Her hands trembled as she wrapped her arms around herself, pressing them tight against her ribs like she could keep herself from falling apart. "I need you with me," she whispered. "In this. In whatever time we have left."

Sebastian let out a sharp breath, raking a hand through his hair. "And then what, Eve?" His voice rose, thick with fury, thick with grief. "I sit by your side and watch you slip away? I hold your hand and count the days? I wait for the moment you close your eyes and never wake up?"

She flinched, but she didn't look away. This was too important for her to backdown on. Her nails dug into her palms as she spoke up. "Yes." Her voice cracked. "That's exactly what you do."

Sebastian exhaled roughly, turning away from her, his hands braced against the wall.

"You don't get to be angry with me for this," Eve said, her voice steadier now, stronger. "You don't get to punish me for something I can't change."

He let out a strangled laugh. "I don't get to be angry?" His hands curled into fists. "You're asking me to watch you die, Eve. You're asking me to sit there and hold you while you slip away. How the hell am I supposed to be okay with that?" He let out a rageful strangled sound. "I am fucking angry!"

"You're not supposed to be okay with this," she said simply. "But I don't want to do this alone."

Sebastian turned to her then, his face wrecked, his breathing uneven. His hands shook as he stared at her, his expression twisted with all the things he hadn't been able to say.

Eve stepped closer. One step. Then another. She sat beside him on the bed, her body weak, her breath shallow, her fingers brushing over the mattress as she tried to find the words. "I know you're losing me," she whispered, watching his face, watching how the truth gutted him. "I know it's killing you. But I'm still here, Seb."

Her hand reached for his, her fingers tracing the familiar lines of his palm, the hands that had held her through everything. "Be with me now," she whispered. "Please. In whatever time we have left, I need you with me."

Sebastian's shoulders trembled. His hands curled around hers for just a moment.
A single, shuddering moment.

Then, he let go.

His jaw clenched as he pulled away, as he stepped back, as he built the wall between them once again. "I can't," he whispered. "I can't be with you while you decide just to leave," he voice filled with rage again.

Eve's heart cracked. "Sebastian—"

"I can't, Eve." His voice broke. "Please… just go back to our room."

Her throat tightened, her chest aching as she looked at him—really looked at him. The man she had loved for half of her life. The man who couldn't bear to watch her fade. She blinked hard against the tears, against the sting of rejection, against the truth she had already known but had refused to accept.

Eve stood slowly, her body weak, her breath uneven. She took one last look at the room that should have been their future. At the man who had been her everything.
Then, without another word, she turned and walked away.

Behind her, Sebastian stayed in the would-be nursery.

Alone.

The Shape Of Fading

Eve had always imagined that dying would feel like something. Maybe it would feel like slipping beneath water, like being pulled under by something heavy and unrelenting, like a slow surrender. But in reality, it felt like nothing at all.

It was not a dramatic breaking apart, no sudden final act. Instead, it was a measured unbuttoning, a slow coming undone, one thread at a time.

It had been a little over a month since she had told Sebastian she was stopping treatment. A little over a month since she had begged him to be with her in what remained of their time. A little over a two weeks since he had asked her to go back to their room and stayed in the would-be nursery.

And now, Eve was still dying. Death was deep in her bones now, closer than it had ever been to it before. She could feel it—not in the way someone anticipates something, but in the way a body knows.

She had lost the weight first.

Her face had thinned, her collarbones now sharp and exposed, her wedding ring slipping from her finger so easily that she had to stop wearing it on her finger and instead kept it on a delicate chain around her neck. Her body had hollowed itself out, her muscles weakening until walking across the room left her breathless, until sitting upright for too long felt impossible.

The nausea never left her anymore. There was no hunger, no craving, no desire for food. The thought of it sat heavy in her stomach, untouched plates piling up in the fridge—meals Maddy had made that Eve just couldn't bring herself to eat.

Pain curled deep inside her now. It was her constant companion. The medication helped, but only just enough. She wore a fentanyl patch which was just enough to keep her from crying out when she moved, enough to make things feel distant and blurry, like she was watching the world through fogged glass.

Her skin had lost its warmth. Even with blankets wrapped around her, even with Maddy tucking them up to her chin, she was always cold now. It was as if her body had stopped trying, as if it had already begun the process of letting go.

And yet, she was still here.

Barely.

But still.

She felt as though she existed in the in-between now, in the space between life and death, in the slow ticking of a clock that would soon stop counting for her.

And Sebastian still wouldn't look at her.

He still moved through the house like she was already gone. Still left the room whenever she entered it. Still avoided her touch, her eyes, her everything.

Eve heard him in the mornings, leaving for work just as she was waking up, slipping out without so much as a goodbye. She heard him at night, the sound of him pacing the floor in the would-be nursery, heard the creak of the mattress as he curled up in a bed that was never supposed to exist.

She wanted to be angry. She wanted to scream, to cry, to demand that he look at her, that he stop making her mourn his love before she had even left him.

But she had nothing left to fight with.

Her voice was weak now, her words slow and quiet, her body too tired to carry grief on top of everything else.

So, instead, she just existed.

She sat in the chair by the window, watching the world outside, watching the wind move through the trees, watching the snow fall in silver spirals to the earth below. She sat there, waiting.

She breathed.

She ached.

She waited.

Because the end was coming, and she could feel it galloping toward her.

This afternoon, Eve was sitting in her chair when she heard keys in her front door. She turned to see Maddy standing in the foyer with a broad smile on her face. She removed her winter clothing and crossed into Eve's living room in a few quick strides. She was holding up a tiny plastic bag like it was a rare, mystical artifact.

"Alright," Maddy announced, shaking the baggie with emphasis. "I had to talk to the very sketchy barista at our café for this, so I really hope you appreciate my efforts."

Eve raised an eyebrow from her chair, her body curled into it like she'd become part of the chair's fabric. "It's legal, Maddy."

Maddy scoffed. "Yeah, well, I like to pretend it's still a little dangerous. Keeps things spicy."

Eve tried to laugh, but her breath caught painfully in her chest, forcing her to swallow down the amusement before it turned into a coughing fit. "Weed's been legal for like five years. You are the least edgy person I know."

Maddy ignored her completely, flopping onto the ottoman near Eve's chair, pulling a pre-rolled joint from the bag with a grand flourish. "Okay, fine. But when was the last time we got high together?"

Eve thought for a moment, tilting her head. "Senior year, behind the high school gym, right before the English final we failed."

"Correction: you failed," Maddy said, lighting the joint and taking a dramatic inhale. She exhaled, then passed it to Eve like a profound offering. "I aced that test."

Eve took the joint, shaking her head. "You wrote a full essay on To Kill a Mockingbird when the exam was about 1984."

Maddy sat up indignantly. "Okay, first of all, I had the spirit of the thing! Orwell and Harper Lee would've been best friends, and I stand by that."

Eve inhaled slowly, letting the warmth seep into her, letting it spread through her limbs like honey. For the first time in weeks, she felt light. Not weighed down by pain, by exhaustion, by the slow shutting down of her body. She exhaled, laughing just a little.

Maddy grinned triumphantly. "There she is."

Eve handed back the joint, stretching her arms out over her head. "It's actually crazy that we survived our teenage years. We were not responsible."

"Excuse me," Maddy said, placing a dramatic hand on her chest. "I was a pillar of responsibility."

"You stole a shopping cart and rode it down a hill into a gas station sign."

Maddy shrugged unapologetically. "And what a smart choice that was! Well, at least it was hilarious."

Eve laughed, full and real, until tears pricked at the corners of her eyes. God, she had missed this. The reckless, ridiculous, dumb things they used to do, the way Maddy could make her laugh until she couldn't breathe. The breathless part came so quickly now.

Maddy leaned back, smiling as she took another long drag before passing the joint back to Eve. "Hey. Remember when we went to that college party, and you threw up on that guy's shoes?"

Eve groaned. "I was fifteen, and your husband, Derrick said it was a movie night! He didn't say it was a literal frat party." Eve squinted her eyes against the rising smoke from the joint as she inhaled again.

"You were so scared of underage drinking that you took two shots and had a full existential crisis." Maddy recalled with a smile, encouraging Eve to take another long drag before handing the joint back.

"It was fireball whiskey, Maddy." Eve put a hand over her heart. "It was like drinking cinnamon gasoline. I thought I was dying."

Maddy wiped a tear from her eye. "You literally sat in the corner apologizing to God."

"It was awful," Eve said wistfully, her voice soft but edged with something almost like reverence. The kind of reverence you had for a time that felt impossibly far away—like holding a seashell to your ear and hearing the faint echo of a life you used to live. There was a longing there, not just for the moment itself, but for the simple, thoughtless way time used to move forward, back when the future felt limitless.

They laughed until their stomachs hurt, until Maddy nearly dropped the joint and had to scramble to save it, giggling uncontrollably.

Maddy was still laughing when she said, "God, remember how you met Sebastian?"

Eve groaned, burying her face in her hands. "Please don't remind me."

"Oh, I'm reminding you." Maddy grinned, her eyes gleaming with mischief. "You were such a disaster. I don't even know how you managed to get him to marry you after that mess."

Eve peeked through her fingers, laughing despite herself. "In my defense, well, I don't have a defence," Eve giggled as she took another long inhale, slowly letting the smoke out of her lungs. "I don't know how I convinced him to marry me either." The effects of the weed blocked Eve from feeling the sorrow of the memory of beginnings juxtaposed with where she and Sebastian were in their relationship now. "I was very hungover that day."

Maddy snorted. "Hungover? You were practically still drunk!"

Eve shook her head, but the memory was already unfolding in her mind, vivid as ever. It had been one of those sticky, late-summer afternoons when the air felt like soup, and the only thing worse than the heat was the head-splitting hangover she was nursing from the night before. She and Maddy had stumbled into that little café near campus, sunglasses on indoors like total idiots, both of them reeking of regret and cheap tequila.

And there he was.

Sebastian.

Behind the counter, sleeves rolled up, hair just messy enough to look like he hadn't tried, but God, it worked. His eyes were this ridiculous shade of warm brown that made her forget how to function. He was laughing at something a coworker said, and his was a laugh that made her forget she felt like she was about to vomit.

Maddy had nudged her, hard. "Go say something!"

Eve had groaned. "Like what? 'Hi, I'm dying, but you're hot'?"

But Maddy, being the menacing matchmaker that she was, had shoved Eve right up to the counter, leaving her there to fend for herself.

When Sebastian finally turned to take her order, Eve had panicked and blurted out the first thing that came to mind: "I'll have... uhh... your strongest coffee. And maybe... your number?"

There was this horrible pause, like time itself had frozen, and Eve wanted the floor to swallow her whole. But then—He'd laughed.

Not in a mean way. Not even in a surprised way. It was this warm, easy, charming laugh that made her knees go weak in a way that had nothing to do with the hangover. "Tell you what," he'd said, scribbling something on her coffee cup before handing it over. "If you survive this hangover you've got going on, text me."

Maddy was practically crying with laughter now. "And you did! You texted him later that night and made me read your message first to make sure you didn't sound too desperate!"

Eve was laughing so hard she could barely breathe. "I was very desperate, okay? But it worked!" She threw her hands up in mock triumph. "Look at us now—married, cancer-ridden, living the dream!" They both dissolved into giggles again, even though it wasn't very funny. Eve's laughter turning into a soft wheeze as she wiped at her eyes.

For a moment, it felt like none of it was real. For a moment, it was just them—two best friends, high as hell, reminiscing about dumb boys and bad decisions. For a moment, Eve wasn't dying.

But then—everything stopped.

Their laughter cut off like a severed string. Eve's vision tilted, warped, folded inward. Her chest tightened, her limbs went numb, and suddenly— the world was spinning too fast.

She gasped.

Her fingers twitched, then went slack.

And then she was falling.

She barely felt herself hit the floor.

Maddy screamed. "Eve!" Her hands were on Eve's shoulders, shaking her, but Eve couldn't answer.

She tried. God, she tried. But her body had betrayed her.

Her lungs forgot how to work.

Her mouth wouldn't move.

Maddy was shouting something, voice high-pitched and panicked, but Eve could only hear the ragged sound of her own breath, the distant echo of the world slipping away.
Everything was too bright, too loud, too far away.

Then—blackness.

The Weight Of Regret

Sebastian arrived home earlier than usual, his shoulders heavy with the familiar weight of exhaustion—a tiredness that wasn't just physical but had burrowed deep into his bones. The hospital had been its usual chaos, a blur of scrubbed hands, sterile hallways, and the rhythmic beeping of machines that measured life in numbers and alarms. But even as he moved through his day, performing the precise, life-saving work that had always given him purpose, his mind had been somewhere else.

Today, he hadn't been able to push Eve from his thoughts. The way she had looked at him in recent weeks—her eyes full of something between resignation and heartbreak—had haunted him through every patient, every procedure. He realized, somewhere between the surgery floor and the hospital's break room, that he couldn't keep going like this. Couldn't keep running. He didn't want to keep running. Not from his wife and what she was going through.

So, he had left his shift early, ignoring the gnawing guilt in his chest as he signed out, trading his white coat for his woolen winter jacket. On the drive home, he had stopped at the flower shop on the corner of Main—the one they used to visit when everything had felt simple and whole—and picked out a bouquet of red carnations. Eve had always loved their bright, defiant colour. They were a symbol of love, admiration... and, today, regret.

As he approached the front door of their home, he exhaled slowly, gripping the bouquet tightly in one hand. Today, he would make it right. He didn't know exactly how, but he knew one thing for sure—he couldn't let her go on thinking he didn't care. Because he did. God, he did.

He had been a coward.

He had spent weeks punishing her for something she had no control over, letting his grief turn to coldness, to avoidance. If he was honest with himself, he had been living in his head, convincing himself that if he stayed angry, if he pulled away, it would somehow make it not real. That her sickness wouldn't be a permanent thing if he didn't look directly at it.

But it was real. And he had wasted time, even when he was perilously aware of how little remained for them.

Tonight, he would apologize. He would sit beside her, hold her, let his lips linger against her forehead like he used to. He would press the carnations into her hands, remind her of all the things she still was to him—his Eve, his heart, his everything.

Sebastian unlocked the front door. He stepped inside, exhaling slowly, already rehearsing what he would say. I love you. I'm sorry. I should have been here. I'm here now.

Then he saw her. Eve was on the floor.

Maddy was beside her, panicked, her hands shaking as she held Eve by the shoulders.

Sebastian froze. The flowers slipped from his fingers.

The carnations scattered across the hardwood, their petals tearing, falling like a blanket of crimson snow. A second passed. Then another. Sebastian's pulse raged in his ears, drowning out everything.

Then—he moved.

He crossed the space between them in an instant, dropping to his knees beside Eve, hands already reaching for her. "What happened?" His voice was sharp, urgent, his fingers pressing against her pulse point before Maddy could answer.

"I—she—" Maddy stammered, her eyes wide, glossy. The room smelled thick with marijuana, the air heavy with it.

Sebastian's panic ignited into fury. "You got her high?" he snapped, shoving Maddy out of the way. "What the fuck is wrong with you? She's dying, Maddy! You thought getting her high was a good idea?"

Maddy stumbled backward. "I— I was just trying to—" In her haze, she could think of nothing to say. She had wanted to help with the pain. She had wanted to give Eve a minute of having her appetite back. She wanted Eve to bite into the delicious peach strudel from their café. It had always been her favourite and she wanted her friend to enjoy it, even if it was just one more time. None of these words came to her. Instead, she let out a giggle.

"Call an ambulance," Sebastian barked.

"I am! I—" Maddy's fingers fumbled as she pulled her phone from her purse, her mind fogged from the weed. When she finally pressed the call button, she giggled again—a nervous, broken sound that had no place in this moment.

Sebastian's head snapped toward her, his expression pure disbelief. "Are you—are you laughing right now?"

Maddy clapped a hand over her mouth, horrified at herself. "I—" Another giggle slipped out, sharp and breathless. "I don't— oh, God, I don't know what's wrong with me."

Sebastian turned back to Eve, his hands moving frantically, expertly. He was a doctor. He had trained for this. But this was Eve. This was his wife. His shaking hands smoothed her hair back, checked her breathing, muttered her name like a prayer.

"I'm here," he whispered. "I'm here, baby. Just hold on."

Eve didn't move.

Sebastian's throat closed up, his voice falling apart as he leaned in closer, brushing his lips over her temple. "I'm so sorry," he whispered. "I don't know where I've been. I don't know what I was doing. I think—" His voice hitched. "I think I thought if I was mad enough, if I ignored it enough, it wouldn't be real. Like I could undo it." He swallowed back a sob, his forehead pressing to hers. "But I can't. I can't undo this. And I can't lose you, Eve. Please. Please, baby. Stay with me."

Maddy's fingers trembled violently as she fumbled with her phone, her breath coming in shallow, erratic gasps. The room felt like it was closing in, the walls too tight, the floor tilting beneath her. She could barely see the screen through her tears, through the haze of panic and THC that clung to her like a suffocating blanket.

She managed to dial 911. When the dispatcher answered, her words spilled out in a jumbled mess. "Uh—uh, my—my friend, she—she collapsed," Maddy stammered, her voice high-pitched, uneven. "She's not—she's not waking up, and I—" She giggled. A sharp, breathless sound that broke something inside of her the second it left her mouth. *Oh God.*

She slapped a hand over her mouth, her eyes wide with horror. *What the fuck is wrong with me?* She scolded herself silently.

The dispatcher was already speaking, calm and steady, asking for the address. Maddy forced herself to respond, choking out the words between gasping breaths and another hysterical laugh that ripped from her throat without permission.

Sebastian shot her a look—pure, white-hot fury mixed with something else, something raw and terrified. He didn't say anything. He was too focused on Eve.

He was kneeling beside her, his hands moving with frantic precision—checking her pulse, tilting her head back, listening for her breath. His fingers trembled, but his mind was on autopilot, falling back on years of training even as his heart splintered with every second that passed.

"Come on, baby," he whispered, his voice cracking. "Breathe for me. Please, Eve. Just breathe." Still, Eve didn't move.

Her skin was too pale, too cold, her body too still beneath his hands.

Sebastian leaned closer, his forehead pressing to hers, his breath ragged. "I'm so sorry," he whispered, the words tumbling out in a desperate, broken rush. The sound of his own voice shattered him, the truth of it settling over him like a weight he couldn't shake.

"I can't lose you," he choked out, his tears falling onto her cheek, mingling with the dampness already there. "Please, baby. I can't do this without you. I won't."

The sound of sirens finally split through the afternoon, growing louder, closer, until they were right outside the house. The flashing red and blue lights bounced off the walls, casting everything in a surreal, nightmarish glow.

Maddy stumbled to the door, flinging it open with shaking hands as the paramedics rushed in.

Sebastian didn't move. He couldn't. It wasn't until one of the paramedics—a young woman with sharp eyes and a calm voice—touched his shoulder that he finally let go.
"Sir, we need to take over," she said gently, but firmly.

Sebastian's hands lingered on Eve's face for a moment longer, his thumb brushing over her cheek as if that small touch could somehow keep her tethered to this world. Then, with a strangled sob, he pulled back.

The paramedics worked quickly, their voices a blur of medical terms and urgent instructions. Oxygen. Vitals. Prepare for transport. Sebastian watched, his body frozen, his mind refusing to process what was happening.

When they lifted Eve onto the stretcher, something inside him snapped. He followed them, his legs barely supporting his weight, his sobs now uncontrollable, wracking his entire body.

"Eve," he whispered, over and over, his voice hoarse, broken. "Eve, please."

Sebastian clung to the side of the stretcher as they wheeled her toward the ambulance, his fingers digging into the metal rails like if he held on tight enough, he could keep her from slipping away.

Maddy trailed behind, her face pale, her eyes wide and glassy. She was still giggling, the sound sharp and hollow in the cold winter air, but tears were streaming down her face now, mixing with the laughter in a way that felt wrong, unnatural.

She knew nothing about this was funny. But her brain was short-circuiting, the weed and the fear twisting inside her until she couldn't tell what was real and what wasn't.

As the ambulance doors closed with a final, echoing thud, Sebastian collapsed to his knees in the snowy driveway, his body folding in on itself, his sobs loud, guttural, unrestrained.

Maddy stood frozen on the curb, her arms wrapped tightly around herself, laughing through her tears, the sound sharp and broken, echoing into the night as the ambulance disappeared down the street, carrying Eve away from them both.

The Quiet Between Heartbeats

The rhythmic beeping of the heart monitor was the only sound in the sterile, too-white hospital room. Eve lay still, her face pale, even against the stiff white hospital sheets, her breathing shallow and uneven. The once-vibrant light in her eyes had dimmed, leaving only the faintest flicker beneath her closed lids. Her skin was cool to the touch, her lips tinged with the faintest blue. The IV drip beside her bed ticked off time in slow, steady drops, a cruel metronome marking the narrowing space between life and what came after.

Maddy sat beside her, clutching Eve's hand with both of hers, her thumbs gently stroking the fragile skin over Eve's knuckles. The warmth was fading from Eve's hand, but Maddy held on. Her own eyes were red-rimmed and swollen, but the tears had long since dried, leaving behind a hollow ache that throbbed in her chest.

The door to Eve's hospital room creaked open softly, and Dr. Patel entered, his face etched with the kind of exhaustion that came from delivering too much bad news. His white coat felt too bright, too clean against the backdrop of impending loss.

Dr. Patel's voice was low, steady, but it carried the weight of inevitability. "Sebastian, can I speak with you outside for a moment?"

Sebastian hesitated, his gaze fixed on Eve's face, as if afraid that leaving the room, even for a second, might cause the fragile thread of her life to snap. But Maddy gave him a small, encouraging nod, her grip tightening on Eve's hand as if to say, *I've got her.*

In the hallway, the fluorescent lights hummed overhead, casting harsh shadows on the linoleum floor. Dr. Patel didn't waste time with pleasantries. "Eve suffered a severe hypoxic event," he began, his voice clinical but not unkind. "Her oxygen levels plummeted, likely due to the progression of the cancer. We believe she experienced a pulmonary embolism—a blockage in one of the pulmonary arteries in her lungs. It's common in advanced cancer patients. We were able to resuscitate her, but it was difficult, and..." He paused, his eyes softening. "Her body is failing. The cancer has metastasized aggressively. She's on borrowed time, Sebastian."

Sebastian's chest tightened, the words sinking in like lead. "What... what can we do?" His voice was hoarse, desperate. "There has to be something."

Dr. Patel shook his head slowly. "At this point, aggressive treatment would only cause more pain. As you know, Eve has already said she doesn't want that. It's time to focus on comfort care." He placed a gentle hand on Sebastian's shoulder. "I recommend transferring her to a palliative care facility, where we can ensure she's as comfortable as possible in these final days."

Sebastian's throat closed around a sob, but he forced it down, his jaw tightening. "I can't... I can't lose her like this. She deserves to be at home, surrounded by the life we built together." His voice cracked, but he clenched his fists at his sides defiantly. "I'm taking a leave of absence from the hospital. I'll be there. I can care for her."

Dr. Patel exhaled slowly, his expression gentle but cautious. "Sebastian... I know how much you want that. But caring for Eve at home won't be easy. She's going to need constant pain management—high-dose opioids, likely a continuous morphine or hydromorphone infusion. You'll need to manage breakthrough pain with additional medication, monitor her breathing, and be prepared for complications like seizures or severe respiratory distress. We'd need to set up oxygen, a hospital bed, and ensure you have 24/7 access to a palliative care nurse. It's a lot to take on, even for someone with your training."

Sebastian's eyes darkened, his voice firm, unyielding. "I know what it takes. I've seen it, I've done it. But this is my wife. I don't want her last days, if that is what we're in, in a sterile room, surrounded by strangers. She deserves to be in her own bed, in her own home, with the people who love her."

Dr. Patel hesitated; his brow furrowed. "Sebastian, you're not just her doctor. You're her husband. This will be different. Watching her slip away—it's not something you can prepare for, no matter how much medical experience you have."

"I don't care," Sebastian snapped, his voice rising before he forced it back down to a level that sounded calm. His eyes glistened with unshed tears. "I need her home. I want to be the one to care for her. I owe her that much." His voice broke, raw and ragged. "I can't let her die in this place."

Dr. Patel studied him for a long moment, then sighed, his shoulders sagging under the weight of what he knew he couldn't change. "Alright," he said quietly. "We'll arrange everything—home palliative care, equipment, nursing support. But Sebastian… you need to prepare yourself. It could be days. Maybe a week or two, at most."

Sebastian swallowed hard, his heart pounding in his chest. "I'm prepared," he whispered, though he knew it was a lie. Nothing could prepare him for an ending. Sebastian closed his eyes, the weight of regret and grief pressing down on him like a physical force. He had wasted so much time—time he would never get back. Time he should have spent holding her, loving her, being with her.

When he returned to the room, Maddy looked up, her eyes searching his face for answers.

"She's coming home," he whispered, his voice trembling with the enormity of what lay ahead. He moved to Eve's bedside, sinking into the chair beside her, and took her hand in his.

"I'm here, baby," he whispered, pressing his forehead to Eve's cool skin. "I'm so sorry. I should have been here all along. But I'm here now. And I'm not leaving your side." Maddy reached across the bed, placing her hand over both of theirs. The room was filled with the quiet between heartbeats, the fragile space where love lingered even as life was slipping away.

In A Room Painted For Beginnings

It had been two days since Sebastian brought Eve home. Two days since he had carried her up the stairs in their home, her weight feeling lighter than it should have been, lighter than it had ever been, like she was already half gone.

He had set her up in the yellow room—the one they had painted when they thought their future was just beginning. A room that was supposed to be filled with the soft coos of a newborn, the gentle rustle of tiny hands against crib sheets, the laughter of a family they never got to build. But now, it was a room for endings.

Sebastian adjusted the nasal cannula resting just beneath Eve's nose, ensuring the flow of oxygen was steady. He checked the morphine pump at her bedside, his fingers moving with the precision of someone who had done this countless times for other patients. But this wasn't just another patient. This wasn't a stranger on his operating table or a name on a chart.

This was Eve. His wife. His everything.

Her skin was pale, almost translucent, stretched thin over the fragile bones of her face. The morphine kept her comfortable, but it dulled her too, pulling her deeper into the fog of sleep. She drifted in and out, her breaths shallow, her body slick with sweat from the fever that refused to break.

Sebastian wiped a cool cloth across her forehead, his hands trembling as he pressed it to her temples. He had done this for children, for infants barely old enough to breathe on their own. But doing it for Eve—the woman he had promised forever to—felt like he was trying to hold water in his hands, watching her slip through his fingers no matter how tightly he gripped.

"Come on, baby," he whispered, his voice hoarse from days without sleep. "Stay with me. Just a little longer."

But there was no response.

Until there was.

Eve stirred, her lashes fluttering against her cheeks before her eyes slowly blinked open. For the first time in days, they weren't glazed or distant. They were clear.

"Seb..." Her voice was a rasp, but there was a spark of alertness, of presence that hadn't been there in the days before.

Sebastian's breath caught in his throat. "I'm here," he whispered, his hand finding hers, squeezing gently. "I'm right here, baby."

Eve's lips curved into the faintest hint of a smile. "You... look like hell."

A broken laugh escaped him, the sound catching on a sob. "Yeah, well... you're not looking too great yourself."

Her smile faded, and her eyes searched his, filling with a depth that made his chest ache. "I'm sorry," she whispered, her fingers attempting to tighten weakly around his.

Sebastian's throat closed, and he shook his head. "No. Don't—don't say that." His voice cracked, the weight of the words unbearable. "I'm the one who should be sorry. I've been... I've been so angry, Eve. At everything. At the cancer. At you. But it wasn't fair. I thought if I pulled away, if I stayed mad, it wouldn't feel so real. Like maybe I could protect myself from this." His voice dropped to a whisper. "But I can't. I can't protect myself from losing you."

Eve's eyes glistened with unshed tears. "I know," she whispered. "I know you've been hurting. But you were never going to lose me, Seb. Not really. I'll always be with you."

Sebastian let out a strangled sob, pressing his forehead to hers. "I don't know how to live without you," he whispered, his tears falling freely now. "I don't want to."

Eve's fingers traced the line of his jaw, her touch feather-light, almost not there at all. "You don't have to know how. Not now. But you will." She swallowed hard, her breath shaky. "I want you to live, Seb. I want you to be happy. I need to know you'll be okay when I'm gone."

"I won't be," he whispered fiercely. "I won't be okay."

Eve's lips trembled, but she held his gaze. "You will," she said softly. "Because you're strong. Stronger than you know." She paused, her eyes fluttering shut for a moment before she forced them open again. "Promise me you'll keep going. For me."

Sebastian's heart shattered. "I can't promise that."

Eve's smile was sad but full of love. "Then promise me you'll try."

He pressed his lips to her knuckles, holding them there like a prayer. "I'll try," he whispered. "For you."

The room grew quiet, the only sound the soft beeping of the monitors and the ragged breaths they shared.

"I love you," Eve whispered, her voice growing fainter, like the words themselves were a struggle to release. "I've always loved you."

Sebastian's tears fell onto her skin, mingling with the sweat on her brow, tracing the contours of the woman who had been his entire world. His chest ached with the weight of everything he had never said, but now, it spilled out in a voice barely holding together.

"I think I loved you from the moment you stumbled into that café," he whispered, his breath catching as the memory burned bright behind his eyelids. "As soon as you asked for my number, all nervous and adorable, I knew. I've loved you every day since, Eve." His voice broke completely, crumbling into a whisper that barely made it past his lips. "I love you more. Always."

Eve's eyes fluttered shut, but her fingers remained laced with his, the faint pressure still there—still fighting, still holding on. Her breath slowed, but it didn't stop. She was still there, still with him, even as sleep began to pull her under once more.

Sebastian didn't move. He couldn't.

He stayed there, next to her, his heart breaking in the yellow room that was meant for beginnings, but had become the place where he was losing her, bit by bit. Not all at once, not yet—but enough to feel like everything was slipping through his fingers.

The house was silent except for the soft hum of the oxygen machine and the faint, laboured sound of Eve's breathing. Sebastian didn't move. He sat beside her, their fingers still intertwined, his other hand resting gently against her cheek, as if he could will her to stay just by touching her.

The front door creaked open, followed by the familiar shuffle of Maddy's footsteps in the hallway. She didn't call out. She didn't need to. She knew where to find them.

A moment later, Maddy appeared in the doorway of the yellow room. She took one look at Sebastian, his face streaked with fresh tears, his shoulders hunched as if the weight of his grief was too much to bear, and her breath hitched in her chest.

Her voice was barely a whisper. "Is she...?"

Sebastian shook his head quickly, his grip tightening on Eve's hand. "She's still here," he whispered, his voice raw and broken. "Just sleeping."

Maddy let out a shaky breath, a flicker of relief washing over her. But it was short-lived. She could see it—the fragility in Eve's shallow breaths, the way her body barely seemed present in this world at all. The end was right there, hovering on the edge, waiting for its moment to pull her under.

Maddy crossed the room quietly, her eyes never leaving Eve's face. She sank onto the edge of the bed, opposite Sebastian, her hand finding Eve's other one, squeezing gently. The warmth was fading, but there was still a faint pulse beneath Maddy's fingertips, a reminder that Eve was still fighting, even if only for a little while longer, with all that her tiny body had left.

Sebastian's breath trembled as he looked at Maddy. The room was too quiet, too heavy with all the things they couldn't say. Without a word, he climbed into the bed beside Eve, careful not to disturb the fragile rhythm of her breathing. His arm wrapped gently around her waist, pulling her close, his face burying into the crook of her neck, where her scent still lingered, faint but familiar.

Maddy followed, crawling onto the other side of the bed, her arms curling around Eve's shoulders, her forehead resting lightly against the crown of her best friend's head.
They lay there, the three of them, wrapped in the quiet intimacy of a love that had been stretched thin but had never broken. The room that was meant for beginnings had become their sanctuary, the place where they held onto Eve with everything they had, even as she slipped further away.

Sebastian's tears soaked into Eve's skin, while Maddy's silent sobs shook against her shoulder. But Eve didn't stir. She was somewhere between this world and the next, teetering on the edge of her ending, but still, somehow, she was theirs.

And in that fragile space, in the warmth of their bodies pressed together, they all drifted into sleep, their breaths mingling, their hearts breaking, in the room that held the last pieces of their forever.

Where Breath Leaves Us And Love Remains

Sebastian woke to a soft wheezing sound.

For a moment, in the fog of sleep, he thought it was just a dream—a nightmare seeping into the edges of his consciousness. But as his eyes adjusted to the dim light of the yellow room, he realized the sound wasn't distant. It was Eve.

Her breathing had changed. It was no longer the soft, shallow rise and fall he had grown used to over the last two days. Now, it was wet, ragged, each inhale sounding like it was being pulled through a thick layer of water. Her chest heaved with the effort, but the breath that followed was shallow, laboured, and unnatural.

It was the sound he had dreaded—the one he knew would come, but had silently begged the universe to spare them. The soft, wet rattle of a breath that no longer belonged to life.

Sebastian's heart clenched in his chest, a sharp, unbearable pain that radiated through his entire body. "Maddy," he whispered, his voice hoarse and trembling. When she didn't stir, he shook her shoulder, harder this time. "Maddy, wake up."

Maddy blinked awake, her face still pressed against Eve's shoulder. For a moment, she looked confused, her eyes searching Sebastian's in the dim light. But then she heard it—the sound—and her confusion melted into horror.

"Is it...?" Her voice broke before she could finish.

Sebastian nodded, tears already spilling down his cheeks. "It's time."

They both sat up, their hands finding Eve's, gripping tightly as if their touch alone could keep her tethered to life. But it was already happening. They could feel it. The end was here.

Eve's body gave a small, involuntary shudder, her chest rising with a strained, fragile breath that sounded as though it had to fight its way free. Her lips were edged with a deepening blue hue, her skin pale and damp beneath Sebastian's trembling hand.

The room filled with a soft, rattling sound—a delicate, crackling whisper that seemed to drift between each breath, as though the air itself had grown heavy inside her. Sebastian knew what it meant. Her body was letting go, her strength slipping away, her lungs no longer able to clear what they once had with ease. He had witnessed this before, in hospital rooms under sterile lights, with patients whose names he had learned but whose lives he hadn't known.

But this wasn't a patient.

This was Eve. This was his wife.

Sebastian pressed his forehead to hers, his tears falling onto her skin. "I'm here, baby," he whispered, his voice cracking. "I'm right here. Just let go. It's okay. You don't have to fight anymore."

Maddy's sobs were silent, her body trembling beside them as she held Eve's other hand, her thumb rubbing circles over the cooling skin. "We love you, Eve," she whispered, her voice barely audible through her tears. "We'll always love you."

And then, it happened.

Eve's chest rose with a deep, gurgling breath—a sound that seemed to pull the air out of the room with it. It was terrifying, a sound that would haunt them both for the rest of their lives.

Another breath followed, shallower, more strained, as if her body was fighting to hold on even as it was giving up.

Sebastian gripped her hand tighter, his sobs now uncontrollable, racking his entire body. "I love you, Eve," he cried. "Please... I love you."

And then came a third breath.

It was the deepest of them all—a long, trembling inhale that seemed to pull from the very core of Eve's being, as if her body was gathering everything it had left for this final release. Her chest rose one last time, shuddering beneath Sebastian's hand, then slowly, quietly, it fell.

For a fleeting, heartbreaking moment, Sebastian swore he could see it—the essence of her, rising from her with that last breath, hovering just above them, suspended in the stillness. It felt as though the very air in the room held her there, lingering at the ceiling, before it finally dissipated into the silence, leaving them behind.

And her chest didn't rise again.

The monitor beside the bed let out a long, flat tone as the line on the screen went straight, Eve's last heartbeat fading into silence.

Eve was gone.

Sebastian collapsed onto her chest, his sobs loud and raw, echoing through the yellow room. "No," he whispered, over and over, as if denying it could somehow bring her back. "No, no, no…"

Maddy clung to Eve's other hand, her face buried against her best friend's shoulder, her tears soaking into the fabric of Eve's shirt. She could feel the warmth fading from Eve's skin, the life slipping away, leaving only the shell of the woman they both loved more than anything.

Sebastian silenced the monitor and the room grew unbearably quiet. It wasn't the peaceful kind of quiet—the kind that follows laughter or lingers in shared, contented silence. This was a devastating, hollow quiet. The kind that echoed off the walls and settled deep into heartbroken souls. The kind that made the absence of Eve's breath feel louder than any sound they had ever heard.

It filled every inch of the room, pressing against their chests like a heaviness they couldn't shake, suffocating them with the enormity of what they had just lost. The air itself felt heavier, like even the house knew that something irreplaceable had slipped away.

Sebastian didn't move. He stayed folded over Eve's still body, his tears soaking into her skin, his face pressed to the place where her heart had once beat beneath his touch. But there was nothing now. No warmth. No rise and fall of breath. No pulse beneath his trembling fingers.

Just silence. Just stillness.

His sobs came even harder, tearing through him with a force that felt like his ribs might crack from the inside out. It wasn't just crying—it was the kind of grief that ripped him apart, raw and primal, shaking his body until there was nothing left but a deep and painful ache where his heart used to be.

Maddy clung to Eve's other hand, her own cries silent but no less painful. She could feel her best friend's fingers continue growing cold againt hers, and there was nothing she could do. Nothing but hold on, even when Eve was already gone.

And in that room—the room they had painted yellow, the room that was supposed to be filled with the sounds of new life—they both felt the crushing, unbearable empty vastness of endings.

It wasn't just Eve they lost in that moment.

It was the future they had dreamed of. The laughter that would never echo down the hallways. The slow lazy mornings and late-night conversations. The life they had built together, now fractured beyond repair. As Sebastian's sobs echoed through the house, mingling with the silence Eve had left behind, it felt like the world itself had come to a standstill.

Because how could time possibly move forward when she wasn't in it anymore?

The Last Light Of Us

To Eve, the world felt distant now—soft and blurred at the edges, like a memory fading before she could fully grasp it. But even through the haze, Eve knew they were there. She could feel Sebastian on one side of her, his hands trembling as they clung to hers, his tears falling warm against her skin. She could feel Maddy on the other, her touch steady, grounding, as if holding on could somehow anchor Eve to this world for just a little longer.

She wasn't awake, not really. But she was aware. And the unbearable sorrow of leaving them behind pressed down on her.

She didn't want to go.

God, she didn't want to go.

She wasn't ready to leave Sebastian—the man who had been her home, her heart, her everything. She wasn't ready to leave Maddy—the friend who had held her hand through every chapter of their lives, who knew her better than anyone else in the world. She wasn't ready to leave the life they had built, the love they had poured into every moment.

But her body was tired.

So, so tired.

And then she heard him. Sebastian's voice, soft and broken, like it was being pulled from the deepest part of him. "I'm right here," he whispered, his breath warm against her ear. "Just let go. It's okay. You don't have to fight anymore."

The words wrapped around her like a balm, soothing the ache in her chest, the fear clawing at her heart. She felt a flicker of relief—that she didn't have to keep holding on, that it was okay to stop fighting.

But she also felt the sharp, searing wish that she didn't have to let go at all. That the light she could feel pulling at the edges of her consciousness wasn't an ending, but a doorway to more life. More laughter. More mornings with Sebastian's arms around her. More late-night talks with Maddy, their laughter echoing.

She held on as long as she could.

For Sebastian.

For Maddy.

But the pull was too insistent.

It was gentle, like a tide slowly pulling her out to sea. But it was relentless. With a final, shuddering breath, Eve felt herself let go.

And in that moment, she felt it—her soul slipping free from her body, rising with her last exhale. It was light, weightless, like the lifting of a burden she hadn't realized she'd been carrying. She floated up, hovering near the ceiling, and looked down at the life she was leaving behind.

She saw Sebastian, his body folded over hers, his sobs shaking him to the core. She saw Maddy, clutching her hand even though Eve wasn't there anymore, her face pressed against Eve's shoulder, her tears soaking into the fabric of her shirt.

She saw the room that was supposed to be filled with new beginnings, now cradling the most painful ending of all.

And her heart ached with a love so profound it felt like it might break her all over again.
But then—Peace.

It wasn't sudden. It wasn't jarring.

It was like light breaking through the darkest storm—gentle, warm, all-encompassing. Eve felt herself burst apart into that peace, into the love she had given and received, into the echoes of the life she had lived.

And even as she dissolved into the light, she knew one thing would always remain.
Her love for them.

For Sebastian.

For Maddy.

And though she was gone, that love would linger in the spaces they had filled together—in the yellow room, in the house they had built, in the hearts of the people who would carry her with them forever.

You've Reached The End But...
The Stories Never Stop

Songs To Stories is exactly what it sounds like—short, emotionally devastating, romantically charged, and occasionally unhinged novellas inspired by the one and only Taylor Swift. Because why simply listen to a song when you can spiral into an entire fictional universe about it?

A new novella drops on the 13th and 21st of every month, so if you have commitment issues, don't worry—you don't have to wait long for your next dose of heartbreak, longing, and characters making wildly questionable life choices in the name of love.

To keep up with the latest releases, visit BrittWolfe.com—or don't, and risk missing out while the rest of us are already crying over the next one. Your call.

See you at the next emotional wreckage.

About The Author
Britt Wolfe

Britt Wolfe was born in Fort McMurray, Alberta, and now lives in Calgary, where she battles snow, writes stories, and cries over Taylor Swift lyrics like the proud elder Swiftie she is. She loves being part of a fan base that's as passionate as it is melodramatic.

She's married to a smoking hot Australian (her words, but also probably everyone else's), and together they parent two fur-babies: Sophie, the most perfect husky in the universe, and Lena, a mischievous cat who keeps them on their toes—and their furniture in shreds.

When Britt's not writing or re-listening to "All Too Well (10 Minute Version)," she's indulging her love for reading, potatoes in all forms, and the colour green. She's also a huge fan of polar bears, tigers, red pandas, otters, Nile crocodiles, and—because they're underrated—donkeys.

Her life is full of love, laughter, and just enough chaos to keep things interesting.

@the.banality.of.britt

BrittWolfe.com

Manufactured by Amazon.ca
Bolton, ON